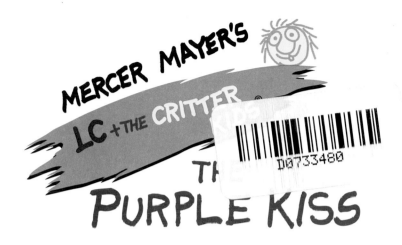

MERCER MAYER'S
LC + THE CRITTERS

TH
PURPLE KISS

A Golden Book • New York

Western Publishing Company, Inc., Racine, Wisconsin 53404

A Mercer Mayer Ltd./J. R. Sansevere Book

Library of Congress Catalog Card Number: 93-80651
ISBN: 0-307-15980-9/ISBN: 0-307-65980-1 (lib. bdg.)   MCMXCV

Written by Erica Farber/J. R. Sansevere

LC

VELVET

LITTLE SISTER

TIGER

KOOL BEAR

SLICK RICK

SU SU GABBY TIMOTHY

GATOR FLEX HENRIETTA

CHAPTER 1

WILL YOU BE MY VALENTINE?

LC crossed his fingers. He was sitting on the bleachers with Gator, Tiger, and other kids who had tried out for the Critterville Hurricane All-Star basketball team. They were in the Critterville Elementary School gym. There were a lot of kids and only four spots left.

LC just had to make the team.

"Gator!" Coach Chili called. Gator jogged to the middle of the court. Slick Rick, the best surfer in Critterville, was standing there with some older kids who had already made the team. LC's hands started to sweat.

"Tiger!" Coach Chili called.

LC high-fived Tiger.

"Henrietta!" Coach Chili called.

LC looked around. There was only one

spot left on the team—and there were still an awful lot of kids.

"LC!" Coach Chili called.

"All right!" LC said, jumping up and running onto the court. He, Gator, Tiger, and Henrietta did the Critter Kid Shake.

"First practice is tomorrow," said Coach Chili. "And practice is what it's all about. Now, Hurricanes, how do you win?" Coach Chili yelled.

LC and all the new Hurricanes yelled back as loud as they could, "Practice!"

"That's right," said Coach Chili. "Practice. So I'll see you all tomorrow."

LC, Tiger, and Gator left the gym together. They started walking home.

"Being on the Hurricane All-Stars is going to be awesome," LC said, dribbling a basketball and passing it behind his back to Tiger. "Hey, I know what we should do. We should practice every day, even on days we don't have practice. Like Coach said, practice is key if we want to win the play-offs."

"Totally!" Tiger said, catching the ball and passing it to Gator. "We'll be the best All-Star team the Hurricanes ever had."

"Yeah," said LC. "We'll go down in

Critterville Elementary history."

When LC got home, he flew into the kitchen. He dribbled the basketball and held it high over his head. *"Air Critter, dynamo dunker, gets set for another three-pointer,"* LC said as he aimed the ball for the doorway. *"He shoots . . . he scores! And the crowd goes wild."*

"LC, you know you're not supposed to play basketball in the house," said Mrs. Critter, walking into the kitchen.

"Yeah," said Little Sister. She and her best friend, Bunny, were sitting at the kitchen table making Valentine's Day cards. There were bits of red and pink paper and lace all over the place.

"Well, today is an important day for basketball," said LC.

"It is?" said Bunny. She looked up at LC.

"That's right. I, LC,

just made the Critterville Hurricanes All-Star basketball team," LC said as he began to dribble the ball. "You happen to be looking at the next . . . " LC paused and held the ball high over his head, ". . . Air Critter." Just then the ball slipped out of LC's hands and bounced against the wall and onto the kitchen table. It knocked Little Sister's and Bunny's cards all over the floor.

"Our valentines, our valentines!" Little Sister yelled. "Mom! LC messed everything up!"

"LC, congratulations on making the team," said Mrs. Critter. "Now, help Little Sister and Bunny pick up their cards. And when you're finished, take that basketball up to your room."

"You get those," said Little Sister, pointing to the biggest pile. "Me and Bunny will get these."

LC moaned as he bent down and began to pick up the cards. "Valentine's Day is for

babies," said LC.

"It is not," said Little Sister. "Dad gives Mom valentines."

"Yeah," said Bunny. "My sister Daisy is older than you and she loves valentines. She gets flowers and candy and lots of really good stuff."

"Right," said Little Sister, nodding.

"Well, maybe Valentine's Day is for girls," said LC. He put the pile of cards on the table.

"Valentine's Day is my favorite holiday," said Bunny, smiling at LC.

"Me, too," said Little Sister.

"LC, you got something in the mail today," said Mrs. Critter. "It's on the counter."

"Oh, yeah?" said LC. He walked over to the counter and picked up a big red envelope. "Hmm," said LC. "Wonder what this is."

"Now, don't forget to bring your basketball up to your room," said Mrs. Critter.

LC ripped open the envelope. Inside was a card with a big red heart on the front.

"Whaddya get?" asked Little Sister. She and Bunny both stared at LC.

"Nothing," said LC, shoving the card into his back pocket.

"What do you mean nothing?" asked Little Sister.

"Just some junk mail," said LC. He grabbed the basketball and ran up the stairs. He went into his room and closed the door. Then he sat down on his bed and pulled the envelope out of his pocket and took out the card again. He sniffed it. It smelled like flowers. Then he opened the card. It said:

BE MY VALENTINE

No one had signed it. At the bottom, there was just a big purple kiss.

LC turned the card over. There was no return address on the front or back of the envelope—just a Critterville postmark. He opened the card again and stared at the purple kiss. He thought as hard as he could, but he couldn't think of any girl he knew who wore purple lipstick.

CHAPTER 2

THE HUNT FOR PURPLE LIPSTICK

Early the next morning LC's alarm went off. He jumped out of bed on the first ring. He was already dressed. There was no time to lose.

"Let's go, Yo Yo," LC whispered to his dog.

Yo Yo wagged his tail and jumped off the bed.

LC picked up his sneakers and his basketball. Then he grabbed a flashlight and tiptoed out of his room, with Yo Yo right behind him. He made his way down the hallway as quietly as he could. Suddenly a door opened.

"Where are you going?" asked Little Sister, frowning at LC.

"I forgot to take out the garbage," whispered LC.

"Right," said Little Sister. "That's why you're carrying a basketball."

"You're going to wake up Mom and Dad," said LC. "Just go back to bed."

"You're going to get in trouble. You're supposed to be in bed, too," Little Sister said as she closed her door.

When LC got to the kitchen, he sat down on the floor and put on his sneakers. Then he tied the flashlight around Yo Yo's neck with a bandanna. He opened the back door and they slipped outside.

"Okay, Yo Yo," said LC. "You stand here and shine the light on the basket."

But Yo Yo wasn't listening. He was running around in circles chasing the light.

"Yo Yo, this is serious," said LC. "Stand right here."

Yo Yo walked slowly over to LC. The light from the flashlight shone on the basket.

"This is Critter Cosell, coming to you live from the Critterdome on the night of the biggest game of the year," said LC. *"A hush comes over the crowd as Air Critter steps up to the paint and shoots."* LC held the ball above his

head, aimed, and threw it. The ball
bounced off the backboard and onto the
driveway. Yo Yo yawned.

"Oh! He misses! But here he comes again,
ladies and gentlemen . . . Air Critter is getting
set for a put-back jam. . . ."

LC dribbled toward the net, jumped up,
and threw the ball. It swooshed through
the basket.

"Air Critter, king of the in-your-face dunk, does it again! The crowd goes wild!"

Yo Yo barked and wagged his tail.

LC practiced shooting until the sun came up. Then he went inside for breakfast.

Little Sister was sitting at the table eating a bowl of Crispy Crispers. Mr. Critter was reading the newspaper. LC sat down and poured himself a big bowl of cereal.

"I knew you were playing basketball," said Little Sister.

"So?" said LC. "I was practicing."

"Yeah, but you're not supposed to practice in the middle of the night," said Little Sister.

"It wasn't the middle of the night," said LC. "It was early in the morning. All the best b-ball players practice all the time, day or night."

"Well, you dropped something in the hallway this morning," Little Sister said, holding one arm behind her back.

"Yeah, what?" LC said.

"Something that's red and smells like flowers," said Little Sister with a big grin on her face.

LC checked his back pocket. The card with the purple kiss was gone.

"LC's got a girlfriend," chanted Little Sister, waving his valentine in the air. "LC's got a girlfriend."

"Give that back to me," LC said.

"LC's got a girlfriend," said Little Sister. She puckered her lips and made kissing sounds. "I bet it's Henrietta. I bet she sent you this valentine."

"Now, stop teasing your brother," said Mr. Critter, looking up from his newspaper.

"Who sent you the card, LC?" Mrs. Critter asked.

LC shook his head. "I don't know," he said. "It doesn't say."

"I remember the first valentine card I sent your mother," Mr. Critter said. "I didn't put my name on it. I just signed it 'your secret admirer.'"

"Oh, dear, I knew it was you all the time," said Mrs. Critter with a smile.

"Well, I have no idea who sent me this valentine," said LC. He took the card from Little Sister and put it in his knapsack. "See you later."

"Have a good day," said Mrs. Critter.

On his way to school, LC decided that no matter what, he had to find out who sent him the valentine with the purple kiss. He just had to know.

When LC got to school, Tiger and Gator

were standing by his locker. "Hey, dude, ready for practice?" asked Tiger.

"Definitely," said LC.

Just then Su Su and Gabby walked down the hall. They stopped in front of Gabby's locker, which was right next to LC's.

"Hey, did you guys hear that we made the Hurricanes?" asked Tiger.

"Great," said Gabby. "We're going to be cheerleaders."

"Cool," said Gator. "We'll all be together."

LC moved closer to Gabby and Su Su and stared at them.

"LC, why are you looking at us like that?" asked Gabby.

"No reason," said LC, looking away. So Gabby wasn't his valentine, and neither was Su Su. Neither one of them was wearing purple lipstick.

LC spent the rest of the day looking for a girl wearing purple lipstick. He didn't see a

single one in any of his classes. Maybe the girl with the purple lipstick didn't even go to his school.

When the last bell rang, LC was the first one in the gym. As soon as the rest of the team had gathered, Coach Chili blew his whistle. "All right, team," Coach Chili said. "Today we're going to do some basic drills—running, lay-ups, dribbling—and then we're going to practice taking foul shots."

After a ton of drills, Coach Chili finally blew his whistle. "Okay, team, it's time for some foul shots. Each player will shoot until he or she misses."

Slick Rick stepped up to the line. He made three baskets before he missed. Gator was next. He made three baskets, too. LC couldn't wait for his turn. He knew he could make *more* than three baskets.

"Henrietta!" Coach Chili called.

Henrietta dribbled the ball for a long time before she shot. She made her first basket and then missed the second. "Sorry, Coach," she said. "I'm a jammer, not a foul shooter. If we were dunking, I could make ten shots, no problem."

"Maybe, Henrietta," said Coach Chili. "But great basketball players must be able to make all kinds of shots."

Tiger was next. LC watched as he stepped up to the line and stuck his tongue out the way he always did when he was  concentrating. Tiger made two baskets and then he missed. LC was psyched. It was his turn. Finally.

LC picked up the ball and dribbled

toward the line. He took a deep breath. He tried to pretend it was just him and Yo Yo in his driveway. He aimed and threw. The ball whooshed through the net. LC was about to take his next shot when the door to the gym opened and Su Su, Gabby, and Velvet walked in with a girl LC didn't know. They were all wearing blue and gold outfits and carrying blue and gold pompoms.

LC dribbled the ball in place and tried to get his concentration back. The girls walked to the other side of the gym. LC aimed and threw. The ball whooshed through the net again. Yes, LC thought, I am a total scoring machine. LC bent his knees and dribbled a few times, threw the ball, and made another basket. And another. And another. And another.

"LC, my main man," said Tiger. "You're on fire."

LC just smiled and made another basket.

On the other side of the gym, Daisy was watching. She didn't take her eyes off LC.

"Daisy," said Su Su. "Will you show me that flip you did again?"

"In a minute," said Daisy without turning around. She was still watching LC.

"Excellent, LC!" Coach Chili said. "Ten in a row. Now that's good basketball."

LC smiled. He felt like he was on top of the world.

"Your All-Star jackets are on the bleachers," said Coach Chili. "You can pick them up on your way out. I'll see you day after tomorrow for our next practice. Don't forget we have our first big game on Friday against the Pirates."

LC walked over to the bleachers behind Tiger and Gator. Suddenly someone tapped him on the shoulder. He turned around.

"Hiiii," Daisy said, batting her eyelashes at him.

"Hi," said LC.

"I'm Daisy," said Daisy, smiling and batting her eyelashes at him again. "I'm the head cheerleader this year."

"I'm LC," said LC. He felt his ears burning.

"I just wanted to tell you that I was watching you play and you've got a great shot," said Daisy.

"Thanks!" said LC. He was feeling pretty good about his shooting himself.

"Well, I guess I'll see you around," said Daisy, staring deeply into LC's eyes.

"Yeah," said LC. He felt himself blushing.

"Well, 'bye," said Daisy. She smiled at LC.

"Ohmygosh!" LC suddenly exclaimed.

"What?" asked Daisy.

"Uh . . . nothing," said LC.

"'Bye again," Daisy said, and gave a little wave. Then she walked toward the girls' locker room.

LC couldn't believe it. He felt like he was going to faint. He couldn't believe his eyes. It couldn't be true. But it was. Daisy was wearing purple lipstick, just like the purple kiss on his Valentine's Day card. What in the world was he going to do now?

CHAPTER 3

SUGAR AND SPICE

The next morning LC was the first one in the bathroom. After his shower, he wrapped one towel around his waist and threw another towel around his neck, just like Air Critter did in his cologne commercial. As LC brushed his teeth, he flexed his muscles and stared at himself in the mirror.

"Looking good," LC said to his reflection.

Just then someone banged on the bathroom

door. "LC, you've been in there forever," said Little Sister. "It's my turn."

"I'm busy," yelled LC.

He opened the medicine cabinet and stared inside. Now that he had a valentine, he figured he ought to smell good. He picked up a bottle of his mother's Critter No. 5. He opened the top and sniffed it. "Yuck!" LC said. "Too flowery."

Little Sister banged on the door again. "LC! I have to go!" Little Sister said. "Hurry up!"

"Just a minute," said LC, his eyes suddenly lighting on a new bottle of Critter Spice on the top shelf of the cabinet. LC brought it down and sniffed. It smelled like cinnamon. "If Air Critter wears Critter Spice," LC said to himself, "then so will I."

"LC, I mean it," said Little Sister. "Hurry up!" She banged harder on the door.

Well, here goes, thought LC. He dabbed cologne behind his ears and then put some on his neck. He sniffed. He couldn't smell anything. He slapped some on his cheeks and then put some under his arms. He figured the more the better. That way he'd be sure to smell good and spicy all day

long. By the time he was finished, he'd used up half the bottle.

LC opened the bathroom door.

"Pee-ew!" Little Sister said, looking at him suspiciously. "What is that smell?"

"What smell?" LC asked.

"You're wearing cologne," said Little Sister. "Aren't you?"

"I don't know what you're talking about," said LC.

"Give me a break," said Little Sister. She walked into the bathroom and slammed the door.

LC got ready for school as fast as he could. After spending all that time in the bathroom, he was running late. He was surprised to see Gabby still waiting for him, standing by his mailbox.

"Since when do you wear sunglasses?" Gabby asked, raising her eyebrows.

"Oh, now and then," said LC. He pushed the sunglasses up on his nose. They were actually his dad's sunglasses and they were a little too big. But he figured they made him look cool.

"Now and then?" said Gabby. "I've known you your whole life and I've never seen you wear sunglasses."

"I guess you just didn't see me when I had them on," said LC. "Oops!" He tripped over a rock on the sidewalk.

"What's that smell?" asked Gabby. She stopped walking and stared at LC.

"Smell?" said LC. "I don't smell anything."

"It smells like oatmeal cookies or air freshener or something," said Gabby.

"I don't smell it," said LC as he started walking faster.

"It's you, isn't it?" said Gabby, catching up to him and wrinkling her nose. "You're wearing cologne."

"Me?" said LC.

Just then someone came up behind LC and grabbed him in a headlock. "Got you!" said Tiger. "Number Two rule of the Ninja: You must have eyes in the back of your head."

"We better go," said LC, hurrying ahead

of Tiger and Gabby.

"Hey, dude, aren't you going to try and get me back?" said Tiger, trying to keep up with LC. "And what is that smell?"

LC just shrugged.

"He's wearing cologne," said Gabby. "Do you believe it?"

Tiger didn't say anything. He just shook his head.

LC kept walking. He was beginning to wish he hadn't put on so much cologne. But it was too late now. He just hoped Daisy liked Critter Spice.

LC didn't see Daisy until lunch. He was on line behind Tiger and Gator, waiting for the next pepperoni pizza.

"What are you going to get for lunch?" LC asked Tiger and Gator.

"Pizza," said Tiger and Gator at the same time.

"Me, too," said LC. He

was just about to reach for a slice of pizza
when someone tapped him on the
shoulder.

"Hiiii, LC," Daisy said. She moved closer
to him and then started to sniff. "Hey, are
you wearing Critter Spice?"

"Well . . . uh . . . " LC mumbled.

"Critter Spice is my favorite," said Daisy.
"It smells soooo good."

LC smiled. "I always wear Critter Spice,"
he said.

Tiger and Gator rolled their eyes.

"So, LC, what are you having for lunch?" Daisy asked. "I'm having the tuna surprise."

"Oh . . . " said LC.

"Everything else has way too much fat in it, don't you think?" said Daisy, looking at LC. "I can't believe anybody actually eats that stuff."

"Uh . . . yeah," said LC. He took one last look at the delicious cheesy pizza and then put a tuna surprise on his tray.

"So, do you want to walk me home after school?" Daisy asked.

"Well, I . . . uh . . . sure," said LC.

"You can pick me up at my locker at three o' clock," said Daisy.

"Okay," said LC.

"'Bye," said Daisy. "See you later."

"Hey, dude, what about our special practice?" asked Tiger, grabbing LC by the arm.

"Yeah," said Gator. "I thought we were going to be the best team ever."

"Missing one practice won't make a difference," said LC. He kept his eyes on Daisy as she slowly walked away.

"Well, I hope you're right," said Tiger. "But remember it was your idea to practice all the time. You're the one who said practice was key."

CHAPTER 4

SHE LOVES ME, SHE LOVES ME NOT

After school Gabby and Su Su met by their lockers.

"So, do you want to practice cheering at my house or your house?" asked Gabby.

"Your house," said Su Su. "You always have the best snacks. I'll ask Velvet to come along."

"Okay," said Gabby. "Did you bring your pom-poms with you?"

"Yep," said Su Su, pulling them out of her locker.

Just then Daisy came down the hall toward them.

"I know," said Su Su. "Let's ask Daisy to practice with us. Don't you think she is like so cool?"

"Yuck!" said Gabby. "I think she's a big phony."

"Hi, girls," said Daisy as she walked up to them.

"Hiiiii," said Su Su. "We were just talking about you."

Daisy smiled.

"Do you want to walk home with us?" asked Su Su. "We're going over to Gabby's to practice cheers for the game tomorrow."

Gabby tugged on Su Su's sweater and frowned at her.

"I'd love to," said Daisy with a big smile. "But I already have a date with someone to walk me home."

"Who?" asked Su Su, stepping closer to Daisy.

"Come on, Su Su," said Gabby. "Let's go."

"Is it someone I know?" asked Su Su.

"Yeah," said Daisy. "He's in your class."

"Does he play on any teams?" asked Su Su.

"Basketball," said Daisy. "He was the highest scorer the other day at practice."

Suddenly Gabby was interested, too. She and Su Su stared at Daisy, wondering who she could be talking about.

Just then LC came around the corner, his knapsack slung over his shoulder.

"There he is now," said Daisy, pointing at LC.

"You're walking home with LC?!" said Su Su and Gabby together.

"Well, yeah," said Daisy. "See you later." She gave them a little wave and walked down the hall toward LC.

"LC? I can't believe it," said Su Su.

"Neither can I," said Gabby. "We've got to save him before it's too late."

"Save him?" said Su Su. "Save him from what?"

"Daisy," said Gabby.

After LC dropped Daisy off at her house, he walked slowly home. He whistled as he came up his front walk. Gabby was sitting on the steps. She jumped up as soon as she saw him.

"Gabby, you're looking good," said LC with a big smile on his face. "Did you do something different to your hair?"

"Look, LC, I've got to talk to you," said Gabby. She sat back down.

"She loves me, she loves me not," said LC, pulling petals off a daisy. He stared into space, still smiling.

"Will you pay attention?" asked Gabby. "This is serious."

"I know," said LC.

"Will you listen to me?" Gabby asked, waving her hand in front of LC's face.

"Sure," said LC.

"I need to talk to you about Daisy," said Gabby.

"You want a daisy?" asked LC, holding out a flower to Gabby.

"Not that kind of daisy," said Gabby. "I mean Daisy, the cheerleader."

LC smiled even more. "Oh . . . Daisy. . . ." said LC.

"She's a big phony," said Gabby.

"No, she's not," said LC. "She's really nice."

"She isn't nice," said Gabby. "You've got to trust me on this. I just have a hunch."

"Hunch, smunch. I know her a lot better than you do," said LC. "And I'm telling you she's really nice."

"No, she's not," said Gabby. "I bet you didn't know that she's only going out with you because you made the most points at practice."

"Gabby, you don't know what you're talking about," said LC. "She likes me. You're just jealous."

"Jealous?!" exploded Gabby. "I am not jealous. I'm just trying to help you."

"I don't need help," said LC.

"You better watch out," said Gabby.

LC just smiled.

"Don't say I didn't warn you," said Gabby. She turned on her heels and stormed down the driveway.

LC pulled the last petal off his daisy. "She loves me," he said, smiling even more.

CHAPTER 5

THE BIG GAME

The next day after school was the big game against the Pirates. All the Hurricanes and the Hurricane cheerleaders piled onto the bus. Coach Chili was sitting in the driver's seat with his clipboard, checking off the names of the players and cheerleaders as they boarded.

LC walked down the aisle to where Tiger was sitting.

"Hey, dude," said Tiger.

"LC!" Daisy suddenly called from the middle of the bus. "I saved you a seat."

"Catch you later," LC said to Tiger.

LC headed toward Daisy. Just as he passed Gabby and Su Su, he tripped and fell.

"You tripped me," LC said to Gabby.

"I didn't trip you," Gabby said without turning her head.

"Then what's your foot doing in my way?" asked LC.

"You weren't paying attention," said Gabby. "You were too busy thinking about Daisy." Gabby kept her eyes straight ahead.

"You're just jealous," said LC. "I'll see you later." He stood up and slid into the seat next to Daisy.

"Okay, let's keep it down," said Coach Chili as the bus rounded the corner by the Pirates' school. "We're almost there."

When the Hurricanes got to the gym, the Pirates were already warming up on the court.

LC watched number 22 of the Pirates

take a shot from the foul line. The ball whooshed right through the net.

"Awesome!" said LC. "That kid is good."

"His name is Bullet," said Slick Rick, sitting down on the bleachers next to LC. "He's the best on the team and maybe in the whole league. He won MVP of the tournament last year. He never misses a shot."

Coach Chili gathered the team into a huddle. They put their hands together, then raised them up in the air and yelled, "Go, Hurricanes!" Then they ran out onto the court.

Daisy, Gabby, Su Su, and Velvet were doing cartwheels on

the sidelines. Then they shook their pom-
poms up and down and yelled:

"*Hurricanes blow with all their might,*
Hurricanes, Hurricanes,
Fight, fight, fight!"

The two teams faced each other.
Henrietta tipped the ball to Tiger. Tiger
dribbled and passed the ball to LC. LC
began to dribble toward the basket. Out of
nowhere Bullet stole the ball from LC,

dribbled down to the other end of the court, and slam-dunked it.

The scoreboard flashed: Pirates 2 . . . Hurricanes 0. . . .

This is going to be a long game, LC thought.

The Hurricanes played as hard as they could. Henrietta even slam-dunked the ball six times in a row. But no one could keep up with Bullet. Even though the

Hurricanes had double-teamed him, Bullet still managed to score an unbelievable forty points!

Meanwhile LC hadn't made a single basket. He didn't know why, but he kept missing. If only he could get the ball again. He knew he could make a basket.

There were twenty seconds left on the clock. The score was now Pirates 42, Hurricanes 41.

"Time-out!" Coach Chili called.

The Hurricanes ran over to the bench and got into a huddle. Su Su, Velvet, Gabby, and Daisy skipped onto the court. *"Give me an H!"* they yelled, shaking their pom-poms high in the air.

"H!" The Hurricane fans yelled back.

"Okay, team," Coach Chili said. "There's only one point between us and the Pirates.

Let's come on stronger than ever in these last seconds. We can win this game!"

"Yeah!" the Hurricanes yelled.

"What have you got?" Daisy yelled.

"Hurricanes! Go Hurricanes!" Gabby, Su Su, and Velvet shouted, doing jumps and cartwheels across the court.

When the game began again, Gator brought the ball out-of-bounds. Bullet stood right in front of LC, guarding him. The referee blew the whistle. LC ran to the right. Then he stopped short. Then he ran to the left. Bullet was gone. LC was open.

"Gator!" shouted LC. "Pass it to me!"

Gator looked at LC and then at the rest of the team. Henrietta was being double-teamed by the two tallest Pirates. Everyone was covered.

"Gator!" LC called again. "Pass to me!"

All of a sudden the ball bounced once on the floor and headed for LC. But before he could grab the ball, it hit him on the head and then bounced off his toe.

"LC, we've got ten seconds!" Gabby screamed.

LC scrambled after the ball. He had to get it. He had to make the shot. Finally he grabbed it and raised it over his head. He took a deep breath. Then he aimed and threw.

"Five . . . four . . . " the crowd chanted.

The ball sailed high into the air, heading right for the basket. It looked like a perfect shot. Suddenly the ball hit the rim and bounced back to the floor. The buzzer sounded. The game was over.

LC couldn't believe it. He had missed. Again.

The Pirates jumped up and down and started to cheer. The final score was Pirates 44, Hurricanes 41. The Hurricanes walked slowly off the court. They went over to their bench, picked up their duffel bags, and headed for the bus. Su Su and Velvet

ere already on board.

"Good game, Tiger," Coach Chili said, hecking off Tiger's name on his clipboard s Tiger got on the bus.

"Nice hustle, Slick Rick," Coach Chili said, patting him on the back.

"High score, Henrietta," Coach Chili said.

"Nice pass, Gator," said Coach Chili.

"Good job of getting open, LC," Coach Chili said, patting Gabby on the back.

"I'm not LC," said Gabby, turning to look at Coach Chili.

"Well, where is he?" asked Coach Chili.

"I bet I know where he is," said Gabby. "I'll be right back."

Gabby ran back into the gym. There was LC, standing in the same spot on the court, staring up at the basket.

"What are you doing?" Gabby asked, running over to him.

"I can't believe I missed the basket," LC said.

"Come on," said Gabby, grabbing LC by the hand. "The game is over."

"But we could have won," said LC. "All I

had to do was make the basket."

"That's okay," said Gabby, handing LC his duffel bag. "It's time to go."

LC followed Gabby out to the bus. He saw Daisy standing in the parking lot talking to Bullet. He couldn't believe his yes. She was wearing Bullet's MVP jacket.

"So, I'll see you Saturday," LC heard Daisy say to Bullet. He watched her smile at him and bat her eyelashes.

Just then Daisy noticed LC. She looked right at him and then turned away.

LC walked slowly toward the bus. "I

guess you were right," he said to Gabby.

"About what?" Gabby asked.

"Daisy," said LC as he and Gabby climbed onto the bus.

"Everyone's invited to my house tomorrow," yelled Su Su from the back of the bus. "I'm having a Valentine's Day party."

"Yay!" everyone cheered except for LC. He just wanted to go home and forget about the game and Daisy and her purple lipstick and Valentine's Day and everything.

CHAPTER 6

THE VALENTINE'S DAY PARTY

It was Saturday afternoon and LC was watching TV. He was still in his pajamas. He still couldn't believe that he had missed the basket at the game and that Gabby had been right all along about Daisy.

Just then the phone rang. Little Sister picked it up. "Phone!" she yelled. "It's Gabby."

"Tell her I'm not here," said LC.

"She said she knows you're here," said Little Sister.

"Tell her I'm in the bathroom," said LC.

"Tell her anything you want."

"She said she's coming over anyway," said Little Sister. "She says you have to go to the Valentine's Day party."

"There is no way I'm going to that party," said LC. But he figured he'd better change his clothes if Gabby was coming over.

LC went to his room and got dressed. Then he went downstairs to the kitchen. Little Sister and Bunny were sitting at the kitchen table counting their Valentine's Day cards.

"Guess what?" said Little Sister. "I got the most cards in our whole class."

"And I got second most," said Bunny.

"Yeah," said Little Sister. "We're the most popular girls. Isn't that great?"

"Great," said LC. He opened the refrigerator and pulled out the milk. He took a sip right out of the carton.

"Hey, don't do that," said Little Sister. "Mom says you're not supposed to drink out of the carton."

"I know, I know," said LC.

"Hey, LC," Little Sister began, "did you ever find out who sent you that Valentine's Day card?" She winked at Bunny.

Bunny waved her arms at Little Sister. "No, no," she whispered.

"Yeah, I know who it was," said LC.

"You do?" said Little Sister and Bunny together.

"Yeah, but she doesn't like me anymore," said LC.

"She doesn't?!" said Little Sister and Bunny, their eyes wide.

"Nope," said LC. "Daisy's moved on. She doesn't like me anymore."

"Daisy?!" cried Little Sister. "Daisy didn't

send you that card."

LC turned around. "Well, then who did?" he asked.

"Tell him," said Little Sister.

Bunny looked down at the floor. "I sent you the card," said Bunny in a little voice.

LC's mouth dropped open in surprise. "You?" he said.

"Yeah, I used my sister Daisy's purple lipstick," said Bunny, her eyes still on the floor.

LC sat down. So Bunny had sent him the card with the purple kiss! He couldn't believe it.

Just then the kitchen door opened.

"Are you ready?" Gabby asked, walking inside.

"Ready for what?" LC asked.

"Su Su's Valentine's Day party," Gabby said, putting her hands on her hips.

"I'm not going," said LC.

"What do you mean you're not going?" said Gabby. "All our friends are going to be there."

"This has been the worst Valentine's Day of my life," said LC.

"Does this have something to do with Daisy?" asked Gabby.

"No . . . well . . . sort of," said LC.

"Forget about her, LC," Gabby said. "Valentine's Day is for friends and fun. Let's go to the party and have some fun."

Just then LC heard a sniffling sound. He looked across the table at Bunny. She was staring up at him. There was one big tear rolling down her cheek.

"Will you go?" Gabby asked, hopping impatiently from one foot to the other.

LC looked at Bunny again.

"Okay, I'll go," said LC,

suddenly getting an idea. "But on one condition. I want to bring my valentine."

"Who's your valentine?" asked Gabby, peering at LC.

"Bunny," said LC.

Bunny started to smile.

"I want to go, too," said Little Sister.

"We'll all go," said Gabby. "Hurry! Everyone's waiting for us."

LC, Gabby, Little Sister, and Bunny ran over to Su Su's house. When LC got there, he looked around at everyone. Gabby was right. Valentine's Day was for friends.